S0-BEB-068

THE
CRACK-of-DAWN
WALKERS

Amy Hest

———————— PICTURES BY ————————

Amy Schwartz

Macmillan Publishing Company
New York
Collier Macmillan Publishers
London

Macmillan Publishing Company
866 Third Avenue, New York, N.Y. 10022
Collier Macmillan Canada, Inc.

Printed in the United States of America

10 9 8 7 6 5 4 3 2

Library of Congress Cataloging in Publication Data
Hest, Amy.
The crack-of-dawn walkers.
Summary: Every other Sunday, Sadie and her grandfather
go for their special early-morning walk.
[1. Grandfathers—Fiction.   2. Walking—Fiction]
I. Schwartz, Amy, ill.   II. Title.
PZ7.H4375Cr   1984   [E]   83-19597
ISBN 0-02-743710-8

For J. G.,
and the crack-of-dawn memories
—A. H.

For Nancy
—A. S.

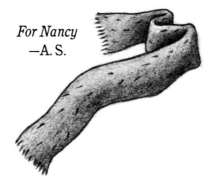

Grandfather taps on her bedroom door. "Are you up?"
he calls softly. "It's time!"

Sadie kicks at the worn pink blanket, and the toasty sheet with stripes. Her feet skim the cold wood floor as she races for the rocker, and the woolen knee socks she left hanging the night before.

"Today is my turn," she sings to herself. "My turn!"

She finds him at the screen door that connects the back porch to outside. "Good morning," she whispers.

"Now you are ready." Grandfather smiles.

Sadie pulls the long purple scarf—the one Gram knit last winter—around her neck. She winds it twice and still the ends dangle below her waist. She feels like a movie star.

"Grandfather," she says, "your hat." She hands over the navy blue beret from "the old country," wherever that was. "No colds this winter," she warns, "and no flu."

"No colds and no flu," he repeats, carefully latching the door behind them.

Snow is thick in the driveway. Sadie is glad she
remembered the warm red boots this time, but later
she will remind her mother how they pinch across
the toes.

"Are you stuck?" she calls to Grandfather.

"We will have to shovel," he answers.

"No, Grandfather!" she protests. "First things first."
She takes his wrinkly hand in her mittened one and leads
him across the street. For his sake she walks slowly.
Grandfather is old.

"I'm glad Ben isn't here."

"And he is glad when you stay behind," Grandfather replies.

"He talks too much."

"Little boys like to chatter."

"He can't keep up."

"His legs are shorter."

"He asks a thousand questions a minute."

"That is how he learns."

"Anyway," Sadie sighs, "a deal's a deal. One Sunday for Ben and the next one for me."

"For me it's a cheat," Grandfather says, "this new deal of yours."

Sadie shakes her head. "Ben and I agreed, for once, that it's best not to share you."

There are four boxy houses on one side of Rugby Road and three narrow ones across the street. Later, when the sun is higher and warmer, the sleepers will creep from their beds and they will press their noses to frosted windows. "Aha!" they will say, spying two sets of snow-tracks. "The crack-of-dawn walkers are at it again!"

Sadie squeezes Grandfather's hand. "Let's pretend you and I are alone in the world."

"No Ben?" he asks.

"No Ben."

"But I would miss him," Grandfather objects. "Wouldn't you, just a little?"

"Not on your life," Sadie answers.

Grandfather inhales the ice air into his old-man lungs. "It was quiet like this in the old country," he says. "Before the troubles."

"I wish I could go with you to the old country."

"It wasn't fancy, like here," he says. "But we were proud."

"Aren't you now?"

"Of course." He smiles. "Old men must be proud."

Sadie pulls the scarf closer around her neck and the hat just below her eyebrows. She wishes she had a furry coat, like the one in Gram's closet.

At Front Street they wait. Leave it to Grandfather never to cross before the light is green, even on a snow-bound Sunday morning. To keep warm she jumps up, then down, then up and down again, first on two feet, then from one foot to the other. Hop, hop. Hop, hop, hop.

Finally, they cross.

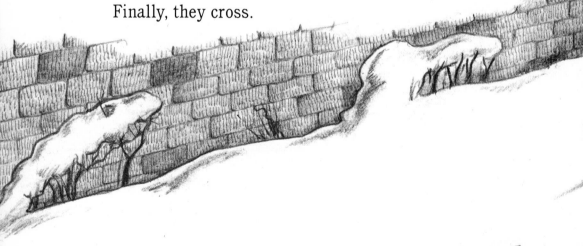

The sign says, "Emma's Bake Shop." Inside, the air is
warm and sweet and smells of fresh-baked bread and
homemade cookies. Grandfather takes a number and when
the hairnet lady behind the counter calls out, "Three," he
waves his hand and says, "Six onion rolls, please."

"Grandfather." Sadie tugs at his sleeve. "Aren't you forgetting something?"

"I don't forget." He winks. "Crumb buns for dessert."

"Because it's Sunday," adds Sadie.

"Yes, it is nice to do a little extra on Sunday."

Outside again, Sadie asks, "Now will we go to Fabio's?"
Grandfather's black eyebrows form two bushy arches.
"Of course we'll go," he says. "Don't we always?"
"Do you take Ben, when it's his turn?"
"He loves to go as much as you."

Sadie wants to hurry, but instead they trudge—through the snow and around those icy patches.

"Did you have candy stores in the old country?" she asks.

Grandfather laughs, very gently. "No candy stores back there," he says. "Like I said, nothing fancy."

"But Fabio's isn't fancy!"

"In the old country," he reminds her, "Fabio's would be very fancy."

Fabio's smells of fresh-brewed coffee, not the instant kind her mother keeps at home. Maybe next year she will sip black coffee with Grandfather, instead of the cocoa with whipped cream swirls.

The long wood counter at the back of the store is cluttered with paper straws and silvery bowls filled with sugar cubes and green relish, ketchup and onion slivers.

Sadie boosts herself onto one of the tall padded stools. She spins around twice to the left, then twice to the right.

"Do you think Ben will be up by the time we get home?" she asks.

"I saw him at the window when we left."

"Was he sad?" Sadie sends the wrapping from her straw sailing toward Grandfather.

"He looked about as sad as you did, at your window, last Sunday."

Fabio wears his starched white apron and a turtleneck
sweater, the brightest shade of red. "One black coffee,"
he says, "and one cocoa, double the whipped cream."
Fabio always remembers.

"We mustn't forget the fat Sunday papers," Sadie reminds Grandfather. "Maybe when I'm older, Fabio will let me stack them at the front of his store."

"Meanwhile, I will help you get one off the top of the pile."

"Does Ben reach the top yet?"

Grandfather shakes his head. "He still isn't tall enough."

"I'm glad."

"One more thing, Grandfather! Suppose we leave a
minute or two for browsing?"

"Why browse?" he teases.

"Just in case I have a yen for something special."

Grandfather laughs. "But you always settle on the bag of licorice, the stringy red kind."

"Maybe one of these days I'll change my mind."

"Maybe," he agrees.

"Today," Sadie announces, "I will give a piece of licorice to Ben."

"How kind!" Grandfather says.

Sadie stuffs the bag into her pocket. "He can have another piece next week," she adds, "even if he decides to stay home."

Grandfather looks surprised. "But next week will be Ben's turn," he reminds her.

"Well, maybe Ben will change his mind."

Grandfather shakes his head. "I don't think so."

"He just may be too sleepy."

"I don't think that, either."

"All right." Sadie shrugs. "But we mustn't forget to say how cold we were today."

Grandfather bends, so slowly, to kiss the tip of her nose. "My guess is that Ben will come next Sunday, my Sadie, and you will stay behind."

"And I will be sad."

"Of course."

"Let's go home to the rest of the family," Sadie sighs. "But for now, Grandfather, we ought to pretend I never have to share you, and that you and I are the only morning walkers."

And they do.